Christmas with Auntie Mary

Eleanor Gormally

First published 2007 by
Veritas Publications
7/8 Lower Abbey Street
Dublin 1, Ireland
Email publications@veritas.ie
Website www.veritas.ie

10 9 8 7 6 5 4 3 2 1

ISBN 978 184730 049 2

Designed by Paula Ryan
Printed in the Republic of Ireland by Betaprint, Dublin

Veritas books are printed on paper made from the wood pulp of managed forests. For every tree felled, at least
one tree is planted, thereby renewing natural resources.

To my Dad, with much love

Auntie Mary lived in a little cottage at the bottom of a hilly field. She had a round face, snow-white hair, soft peachy cheeks and huge hugging arms.

Every year, without fail, on Christmas Eve little Liam and Emer went on a visit to their Auntie Mary. They always came early and left before dusk.

This year the snow began to fall as Emer and Liam crossed the fields behind their house and headed for Auntie Mary's cottage. Tucked inside the red rucksack on Emer's back were presents, all done up in bright, glittery paper.

'There you are are,' Mary beamed, as she lifted the latch to let them in.
'I thought you'd never get here!' Emer and Liam bounced
excitedly in the door, making the not-so-round holly
wreath go wibble-wobble.

'We brought you presents!' they cried. Auntie Mary laughed as she took
the bundle of sparkling paper and carefully unwrapped her parcel. Pink smelly soap and a
jar of white, gooey face cream! All the while, the snow continued to fall silently.

Liam and Emer loved these Christmas visits. They loved the not-so-round holly and ivy wreath that swung from the front door.

They loved the tall, tilting Christmas tree that stood in the hall. They loved the smell of the turf fire in the snug kitchen. But most of all they loved Auntie Mary's stories!

Emer pulled off her woolly gloves and warmed her hands by the open fire. The snow fell thick and heavy. Liam searched for sweets hidden by Auntie Mary all around the cottage. The snow piled higher and higher against the door and windows. And no one noticed.

'**Wow!** Look at the snow,' Liam shouted, flattening his nose against the cold window when it was time for them to go home. Auntie Mary looked out at the glistening white blanket. 'There's no going home in that,' she said. 'It might be better if you two stay the night with me.'

Tears ran down Liam's chubby cheeks. 'What about Santa?' he cried. Then thinking of his Christmas stocking he sobbed even louder. 'I want to go home, NOW!' Even Auntie Mary's sweets didn't help! Emer hugged little Liam close to her. 'Don't cry, Liam,' she said, poking her freckled face into his. 'Santa will know where we are! Just wait and see!'

'How about we go out and check the animals, Liam?'
Auntie Mary asked, as she took his small hand in hers. And wrapping him in one of her old
coats they trudged together through the snow. 'Can't forget the poor cows and the
donkey tonight of all nights,' she said, handing Liam a fistful of hay.

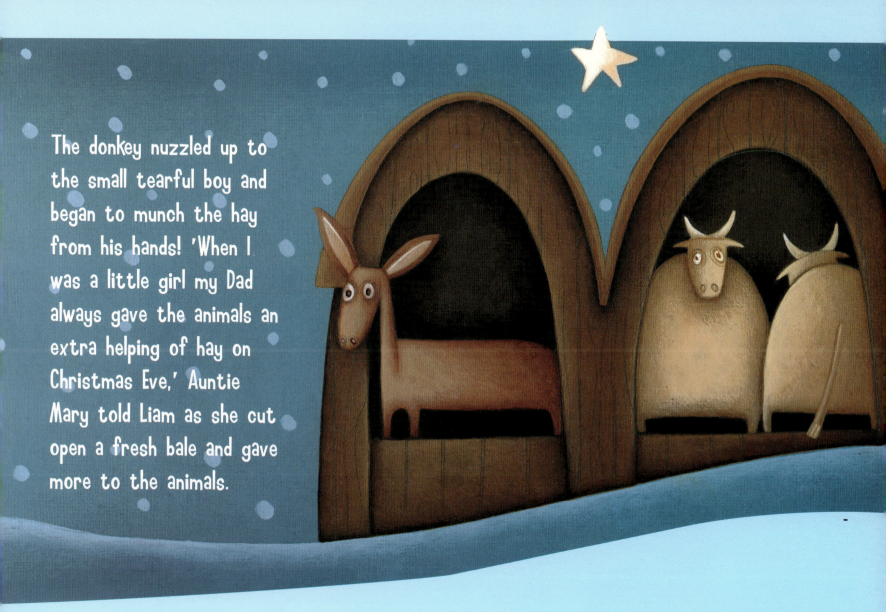

The donkey nuzzled up to the small tearful boy and began to munch the hay from his hands! 'When I was a little girl my Dad always gave the animals an extra helping of hay on Christmas Eve,' Auntie Mary told Liam as she cut open a fresh bale and gave more to the animals.

'It's lovely and cosy in here,' said Liam. 'Sure if it wasn't for the heat of the animals,' Auntie Mary replied, 'how would Mary and Joseph have managed to keep Jesus warm that first Christmas night?' Liam giggled as he thought of a baby snuggling up to a COW and a donkey!

Emer stayed inside the cottage. At first she played with the musical crib that sat on the windowsill. Then she watched out for signs of Santa's sleigh. At last she heard Auntie Mary and Liam come in from the barn.

There were bits of hay sticking out of Liam's hair but there was no sleigh or reindeer or red-cloaked, white-bearded man in sight. Feeling a bit disappointed, Emer turned to her aunt and asked what she had been waiting to ask all evening. 'Will you tell us one of your stories? Please?' Auntie Mary's eyes twinkled with anticipation. 'Of course I will, love,' she smiled, 'but first let's open some of our treats.'

In the soft glow of the tidy kitchen, Emer watched in amazement as Auntie Mary took a large brown box from above the cupboard and placed it carefully on the table.

'What's that?' Liam shouted with excitement. 'A Christmas Box,' Auntie Mary said. 'A present that has come from old Mr Burke's shop down in the village every Christmas for as long as I can remember.' The children craned their necks to peep in. 'You're usually gone home by the time I open it,' she said. 'Now, let's see what we have this year.' Auntie Mary let the children take turns at pulling out the treats: ham dotted with spicy cloves, a turkey all ready for the oven, a fat, round plum pudding, rosy red raspberry jam in a bubbly glass container, chocolate biscuits, toffee sweets and the cutest Christmas cake that had not one, but **three** snowmen sunk into the white icing! The table was laden with the most amazing treats the children had ever seen.

Auntie Mary stopped and looked around her neat kitchen, at the table full of food, at the children, their eyes gleaming with delight. She smiled to herself. This was going to be a grand Christmas. An eager hand tugged at Auntie Mary's apron. 'You haven't forgotten about our story?' Emer pleaded, her cheeks pink with excitement 'Of course I haven't,' she reassured her. 'Let me pull the couch over close to the fire.'

The children snuggled down between the cushions and watched her as she stoked the turf in the grate and put the Christmas candle by the window.

At last all was in place for the children to hear Auntie Mary's special story.

'This is a story,' she began in a hushed and low voice, 'about
a woman called Mary, a man called Joseph and a little baby
who was about to be born.'

'This is no ordinary story,
it is an extra ordinary story
an ancient story ... a story that has been told for over two-thousand years.
A story told to me by my mother when I was your age,' she smiled at the children.

'And it all began on that special night ... fadó, fadó.'

'Some said it was a beautiful night.
The sky was dark and soft and velvety
and teeming with tiny stars.
Some said that a light hung in the sky
like shimmering sparkling dust.
Some said something mysterious and
magical was about to happen.'

The little kitchen became quiet and still.

'Well, on that night Mary and Joseph were in Bethlehem. They had trekked all the way from the village of Nazareth. Their emperor, Caesar Augustus, wanted to know how many people lived in his kingdom, so Mary and Joseph had to travel all the way to Bethlehem — back to where Joseph's people came from — to sign a big book.'

'But when they arrived, Bethlehem was crowded. Women, children and men were everywhere, all looking for somewhere to stay. There was no room left in any of the local inns, which wasn't very good news as it was getting near the time for Mary's baby to be born.'

'Poor Mary,' Emer said. 'I hope she'll be ok.'
'Oh, don't you worry, love,' Auntie Mary said confidently, 'God always looks after us!'

'Now nobody knows for sure how they found a place, but find a place they did, and so the story goes that in the warmth of a stable Mary gave birth to a boy. She wrapped her little treasure in swaddling clothes and put him to sleep in a manger.'

'And the cows and donkey kept him warm!' chirped Liam.

'But what about the shepherds?' Emer asked excitedly, taking the musical crib down from the window. 'They're on their way,' Auntie Mary said softy. Emer shut her eyes tight and sure enough she could see the shepherds coming down from the hills, one by one. 'Down they came with sheep and lambs,' Auntie Mary said, gazing into the fire, 'and what amazing stories they had about angels, dazzling lights and sweet singing.'

'They had left their fields in search of a baby that the angels had told them would be wrapped in swaddling clothes and lying in a manger. And there he was! Our very own Saviour.'

'And the wise men brought all their presents,' Liam shouted eagerly, as he eyed all the goodies.

'Indeed they did!' said Auntie Mary. 'They came from the East, you know. They were looking for a baby too! First they went to Jerusalem. But the baby wasn't there. Then a bright star pointed them to Bethlehem. They arrived with wonderful gifts of **myrrh** and **gold** and **frankincense**. They bowed before the baby and then walked quietly into the night.'

'What a funny thing to do!' laughed Liam. 'I think Mary might have thought so too,' his aunt nodded. 'She knew something very special was happening. So she treasured in her heart everything she saw and heard that night.'

Suddenly the little kitchen filled with the soft sound of
'Silent night, Holy night'.
It was coming from the musical crib!

Auntie Mary hugged the children close. 'Never forget,' she whispered, her voice soft and serious ...

'This is no ordinary story......

it is an extra ordinary story,
a story told for over two-thousand years.
A story told to me by my mother.
A story you can tell too!'